PUFFIN B

ALEX AND THE IC...

Yvonne Coppard was born in Ruislip, Middlesex, in 1955, the fourth of five children. Before becoming a full-time writer, she taught in London, Plymouth and Ely, then worked in child protection with the Cambridgeshire Local Education Authority. Married with two daughters, Yvonne lives just outside Cambridge. She loves reading, cinema, swimming, gossip (though not the vicious variety) and old buildings.

Books by Yvonne Coppard

ALEX AND THE ICE PRINCESS
WHAT'S COOKING, ALEX?

Look out for

ALEX IN WONDERLAND

ALEXANDRA THE GREAT

Alex and the Ice Princess

Yvonne Coppard

Illustrated by Jan McCafferty

PUFFIN

PUFFIN BOOKS

Published by the Penguin Group
Penguin Books Ltd, 80 Strand, London WC2R 0RL, England
Penguin Group (USA) Inc., 375 Hudson Street, New York, New York 10014, USA
Penguin Group (Canada), 10 Alcorn Avenue, Toronto, Ontario, Canada M4V 3B2
(a division of Pearson Penguin Canada Inc.)
Penguin Ireland, 25 St Stephen's Green, Dublin 2, Ireland (a division of Penguin Books Ltd)
Penguin Group (Australia), 250 Camberwell Road, Camberwell, Victoria 3124, Australia
(a division of Pearson Australia Group Pty Ltd)
Penguin Books India Pvt Ltd, 11 Community Centre, Panchsheel Park,
New Delhi – 110 017, India
Penguin Group (NZ), cnr Airborne and Rosedale Roads, Albany, Auckland 1310, New Zealand
(a division of Pearson New Zealand Ltd)
Penguin Books (South Africa) (Pty) Ltd, 24 Sturdee Avenue, Rosebank, Johannesburg 2196,
South Africa

Penguin Books Ltd, Registered Offices: 80 Strand, London WC2R 0RL, England

www.penguin.com

First published 2005
1

Text copyright © Working Partners Ltd, 2005
Illustrations copyright © Jan McCafferty, 2005
All rights reserved

The moral right of the author and illustrator has been asserted

Set in 11.5/16pt Adobe Leawood
Made and printed in England by Clays Ltd, St Ives plc

British Library Cataloguing in Publication Data
A CIP catalogue record for this book is available from the British Library

ISBN 0-141-31803-1

To Jessie, with love

Chapter One

'**O**ver here, Alex!'
I turn graciously to the waiting cameras.
'What a supermodel!' murmurs one reporter
to another as the cameras pop. 'So fresh!'
'Do that thing with your specs,
Alex!' calls a photographer.
I sigh in a good-humoured way
and nudge my glasses back up my nose with a
casual flick of my hand. It's such a responsibility
being the next big
thing.
I smile at
the chauffeur
and sweep into
my limousine, turning to
Rosie, my best friend, personal assistant and
stylist. 'Remember the old days? When I think of

the hours I used to spend painting lemon juice on my face to make the freckles fade, and hating my hair . . .'

'I know,' laughs Rosie. 'Now everyone is painting on freckles and copying your "windswept" hairstyle. It's amazing.'

'Alex . . . Alex! One last picture! Over here!'

I turn again to the cameras. 'This is definitely the last one!' I laugh.

'Last one what?' Rosie asked, looking confused. 'Are you on some other planet – again?'

I thumped back into reality. I was not in a grand limo; I was in assembly, sitting cross-legged on the school-hall floor. Rosie was not my glamorous and sophisticated personal stylist; she was in Class 6 at Derrington Primary, just like me. And there was definitely nothing glamorous and sophisticated about the stain on her T-shirt where her baby sister had slobbered over her.

'Where were you this time?' Rosie grinned. We've known each other since nursery, so she's used to my daydreams.

'Just planning my future,' I said.

Miss Ross, our head teacher, was still in full flow. She was talking about our Winter Fair. It was to raise funds to buy new books and computers and stuff for the school, and it seemed like the whole of Derrington was getting involved.

'There will be refreshments and a jumble sale here in the school hall,' Miss Ross went on. 'Cake stalls and game stalls, along with face-painting, ice creams and candyfloss will all be in the playground. And so will demonstrations from the local fire brigade and first-aid organization.'

'Stop, stop, I'm going to faint with all the excitement,' muttered Rosie.

I giggled.

Miss Ross's face was set like concrete as she turned her gaze on me. 'Would you like to share the joke with us, Alexandra Bond?' she asked.

'Er, no, Miss,' I answered, shuffling uncomfortably.

Miss Ross pursed her lips. 'Now, one of the most exciting things,' she went on, 'will be our Winter Parade. The school will lead the parade

– followed by all the local organizations and businesses taking part on specially decorated lorries and floats. Everyone in the school – children *and* teachers – will wear a costume.'

A murmur of excited chatter broke out.

'Our theme is "Storyland",' Miss Ross continued, 'so your costumes will be based on a favourite story or poem. And, after assembly, your teachers will tell you how you're going to make your costumes.'

Miss Ross then beamed her special smile, the one she usually keeps for Christmas. 'There's even more exciting news for Class Six,' she said. 'The Class Six pupil with the most imaginative costume will lead the Winter Parade.'

The chattering in the Class 6 row grew louder.

'I know all about this already,' said Pearl Barconi smugly. 'It was my mother's idea.'

Pearl Barconi is my sworn enemy. Me and Rosie call her Macaroni because her Italian granddad got very rich from selling pasta. And also because it annoys her.

'Your mother organizes everything,' said Liam Miller. 'Anything to get her face in the paper, my dad says.'

Pearl's fan club (three silly girls in our class who think Pearl is some kind of superstar because her mum used to be a model) scowled like mad.

'Amber is very generous with the time she gives to charity work. Everyone says so,' Pearl said frostily.

Macaroni calls her mum by her first name. How weird is *that*?

'All right, settle down,' said Miss Ross sternly, and looking pointedly at Pearl. 'Everyone will be given a letter to take home this afternoon with all the details. Make sure it goes straight to your parents and does not linger in the bottom of your bag. Remember, the whole community of Derrington is pulling together for our school's benefit. We must all play our part. And you can start, Susanna Riley, by taking your hand out of that pocket where you're hiding sweets, and seeing me after assembly.'

Susanna Riley went bright red and everyone else looked over in sympathy. Miss Ross has radar for sweets – and for chewing gum, even if you leave it in your mouth and never chew it while she's looking. That's why she's the head teacher.

Back in class, Miss Westrop explained a bit more.

'You are going to be designing and making your costumes here in class,' she said, 'although you may want to get a bit of help from home with them as well. So you need to get thinking right away about what kind of costume you would like to make.'

'Can our costume be from a comic book, Miss?' Dominic asked. 'That counts as a kind of book, doesn't it?'

Miss Westrop nodded. 'And you can adapt clothes you already have: cut them and sew them into different shapes, dye them a different colour, or sew decorations on them – anything you like.'

'I already know what my costume is going to be,' Pearl piped up. 'And it's going to be great.'

'I bet you'll win, Pearl,' simpered Melissa, one of Pearl's sidekicks.

'Yes, well, I'm sure that everyone is going to try their hardest to produce some wonderful costumes,' continued Miss Westrop with a slightly annoyed expression on her face. 'And remember – the best costume will not necessarily be the most expensive to make, or the most beautifully sewn. It will be the most *imaginative* – the one with a really clever idea behind it.'

Sewing may not be my thing, but having clever ideas definitely is. I looked across at Rosie and she grinned. I just knew she was thinking the same as me!

At morning playtime, everyone was talking about the Winter Parade. Rosie and I got straight down to planning.

'I don't care who wins as long as it's you or me,' I said. 'And definitely NOT Macaroni,' I added as Pearl came sauntering across the playground towards us, her fan club in tow.

'Any costume ideas yet?' Macaroni asked.

'None that we want to tell anyone about,' I said airily.

Macaroni smirked. 'I see. No ideas yet. Don't spend too much time on it. I'm afraid my costume is already on its way. Trust me, your chances aren't that great.'

'And yours are, I suppose,' I replied, trying to sound completely uninterested.

'Well, I do have the advantage of experience in parades and competitions,' said Macaroni smugly. 'Remember, I won the Pretty Miss Bognor contest.'

'Were you the only contestant, then?' asked Rosie.

Macaroni gave Rosie a look, then flounced off, tossing her hair. The fan club did the same.

Rosie and I rolled our eyes at them.

'I wonder what Pearl's costume idea is,' Rosie said glumly, after they had gone. 'I bet it's really stylish.'

'But Macaroni's only got style because she wears whatever her mum tells her to,' I snorted. 'You heard what Miss Westrop said. They're looking for imagination – and Macaroni has the imagination of a bag of frozen peas – *so* we *must* be in with a chance!'

'*And here to present the Alexandra Bond Award for the Most Imaginative Design is the person who the award was named after.*'

I step forward to the microphone in my

one-of-a-kind dress, designed especially for the Fashion Awards. 'Thank you so much, it's an honour to be here. I never thought that one day I would win an award for my designs, let alone have one named after me!' I say to the captivated audience. 'Who could have thought that my costume design for my school's Winter Fair would go on to inspire lookalikes around the world and an entire trend in fashion? But I am delighted to be here . . .'

Chapter Two

Back at home, my five-year-old brother, Evan, was bursting with his own news about the Winter Fair. 'Everyone in Class One is going to be an elf!' he yelled.

Bear, our big Newfoundland dog, wagged his tail and barked. He didn't know what the excitement was about, but I could tell he hoped there might be a sausage or a biscuit involved.

Dad emerged from his study to see what was happening. Mum told him it was news about the Winter Fair. He looked a bit confused. He's a writer and he doesn't come out of his study much.

'I'm going to have a song to sing and

everything!' Evan puffed his chest out proudly.

'And Class Six are having a costume competition,' I said. 'The person with the most imaginative costume will lead the whole parade and –'

'And elves are going to be in the parade!' interrupted Evan. 'I'm going to be an elf, Mummy!'

Mum nodded. 'Yes, Evan, so you've said. Let your sister finish.'

I went on with my news. 'So I need a really, really good costume, because I want to lead –'

'And *I* need a costume too,' said Evan, 'because I'm going to be –'

'Upside down in the dustbin, if you don't keep quiet for a minute,' I said in frustration.

Evan looked at me with wide-eyed innocence. He was good at that look, but it didn't fool me. I don't call him Evan the Terrible for nothing! It's no surprise to me that my name goes with something fantastic (like Alexander the Great, this legendary warrior and leader) and Evan's goes with something awful (like Ivan the Terrible, this really scary guy from Russian history).

'Who's making these costumes?'

asked Mum suspiciously. She hates sewing.

'Don't know about Evan's, but for mine –' I handed her my letter.

'Did your teacher give you a letter to bring home too, Evan?' asked Mum.

'Can't remember,' Evan replied.

Mum rummaged in his bag and pulled out a letter. 'Yep, here it is. Oh, thank goodness,' she said, reading it. 'A couple of parents are going to make all the elf costumes. Ahhh . . . The children will be making their own little elf hats in class. That's sweet.'

'We're making our own costumes in class too,' I said, to bring everyone's attention to where it should be – on me. 'I just need an old dress or something, and stuff to decorate it with.'

Mum raised her eyebrows. 'What, you mean, *you're* going to sew?'

'Yes,' I said, imagining myself putting the finishing touches to my latest sensational creation – effortlessly produced by my newly discovered skill with a needle and thread.

'Are you sure that's a good idea?' Mum asked dubiously.

'If you're thinking about that time I sewed

my Barbie's scarf to the tablecloth, I was really little then,' I said defensively.

'Mmm, I'd forgotten that one,' said Mum. 'I was thinking more of the buttons you sewed on top of the buttonholes to save time, as you put it. And the poor teddy bear with arms longer than his legs . . .'

'Yes, all right, there's no need to go on,' I snapped. 'We can have help. I expect Rosie's mum will give me a hand. *She's* very good,' I added pointedly.

Mum looked suitably crushed as I flounced out of the room to work on my idea.

When I say 'idea', that's a bit of an exaggeration.

I didn't have one yet.

After half an hour or so of unsuccessful hard thinking, I slunk despondently down the stairs and flopped on to the sofa next to Dad and Evan. Dad had taken a break from his writing to watch *Rocket Boy* – which I think he enjoys even more than Evan does.

But as Rocket Boy zoomed from galaxy to galaxy, doing heroic deeds for all mankind, an idea formed in my mind. All I needed was my old swimming costume and plenty of silver foil . . .

I worked on my idea in my bedroom until bedtime, and got up early the following morning too – even though it was Saturday. I'd almost finished it when Rosie rang on the doorbell.

Dad let Rosie in and called up the stairs to me. 'You can come out now, Alex. Your partner in crime is here!'

I heard Rosie groan and giggle. Carefully, I opened the door and wobbled my way across the landing to the top of the stairs.

'*Whoah!*' said Dad as he saw me. 'What on earth . . .'

'Alex! You're a . . . um . . . What are you?' Rosie stumbled.

I looked down at them and swept my arm in a wide arc, showing an imaginary scene. 'Picture darkness . . . Picture bright silver stars . . . The cold metal of the spaceship . . . Two perfect silver moons . . .'

'What?' Rosie asked, mystified.

'We're on another planet, obviously,' I said impatiently.

'We certainly are,' Dad agreed.

'Descending from her galactic patrol ship comes –' I did a trumpet fanfare sound – 'the Star Warrior!'

I started to come down the stairs. It wasn't easy. As soon as I moved, my hastily constructed silver-foil warrior helmet started to slip off. It was tall and pointy, with two silver horns and little foil stars that seemed to float out of their tips. I hoped Dad wouldn't realize I'd straightened all his paper clips to hang the stars from.

Holding on to the helmet I started again. At least my silver skirt and belt stayed in place (more silver foil with transporter and weapon controls made of sweet wrappers – it was a sacrifice, having to eat so many so soon after tea, but you have to suffer for your art).

'It's . . . er . . . great, Alex . . .' said Rosie, sounding a little less overwhelmed with admiration than I had hoped. 'I wonder, though, if the, um, hat thing will stay on. It looks very tall . . .'

'Too tall,' said Dad. 'One puff of wind, or a sudden turn, and it'll fly straight off.'

'No, it won't,' I said indignantly, and took another step towards them. The helmet was sliding like mad, but I hung on to it determinedly.

'I hope that's not my baking foil,' Mum warned as she came out into the hall with Evan in tow.

I pretended I hadn't heard.

'Your hat's falling off,' Evan said, helpfully pointing at it.

'It's a helmet,' I said. 'And it isn't falling –' The helmet slid off my head and rolled down the stairs, hitting each step as it went.

'It *is* my baking foil,' said Mum, peering at it.

'Er, sort of,' I muttered.

'Er, it is *exactly* my baking foil!' Mum corrected. She shook her head. 'Alexandra Bond, what a waste. It won't even stay on.'

'Of course it will,' I said hotly. 'This is only a practice version – I'll make a better one at school.'

'The belt's nice – can I have a go?' asked Evan.

'Sure, Evan,' I said generously. 'And the helmet too,' I offered, pleased that someone appreciated my creativity – clearly my little brother isn't *all* bad.

'I don't want to try *that*!' he said.

Or maybe he is.

'It's very unusual,' Rosie said supportively.

'But it won't work!' said Mum and Dad together.

Honestly, some people have no vision. 'We'll see, shall we?' I said. 'Come on, Rosie, we'll take it on a test run up to Mrs Runce's shop.'

'Are you sure?' Rosie asked doubtfully.

I nodded, then crammed the slightly crumpled helmet back on to my head, bending my neck a bit to one side to help it balance.

The helmet fell off five times on the way to Mrs Runce's shop and, of course, Melissa, one of the simpering Macaroni fan club, had to be walking down the street at the same time.

She stood watching with her mouth open as Rosie and I passed.

We ignored her.

'Oh, my dear, what have you got on?' asked Mrs Runce as we went into the shop.

'It's a test costume,' I told her. 'For the Winter Parade.'

'I see,' said Mrs Runce. 'Maybe this will help,' she added, giving me a free chocolate bar. In other words, she didn't think it would work either.

On the way back, we passed Melissa again. But this time, somehow, she had Macaroni with her.

'Hey, Alex! That's not your costume, is it?' Pearl laughed as the helmet fell off again. The point was completely bent now and the silver horns were facing the wrong way.

'Not that it's any of your business,

Macaroni,' I said, 'but I'm just testing out some ideas. This isn't the finished thing.' I haughtily bent down to pick up my helmet – and as I did so my silver skirt fell off too.

I hastily swept it up and grabbed Rosie's arm. 'Come on, Rosie.' And we sped off, me trying to look as if walking up the street in your swimming costume was perfectly normal.

Chapter Three

As I'd suspected, Macaroni and her fan club made the most of my embarrassment. When Rosie and I arrived at school on Monday morning, they were whispering behind their hands to people and helpfully pointing me out.

A group of boys from my class came up to me in the playground. 'Pearl says you've got a really freaky costume made out of tinfoil – is that true?' one of them said. 'Can we see it?'

'I don't know what you're talking about,' I replied sniffily.

'Pearl says you look a bit like a helicopter gone wrong in it . . .' said someone else. The group all sniggered.

'You should know better than to listen to anything Macaroni Barconi says,' Rosie said haughtily, and we swept off like we didn't care at all.

But I was hopping mad, and Macaroni's sickly sweet smile when she saw me coming into class didn't help.

'Hello, Alex. How's the heli– I mean costume coming along?' she asked.

I ignored her, but I knew everyone was picturing me in a stupid, stupid, tinfoil suit, and laughing to themselves. That made it even more important to come up with something totally brilliant for the parade.

'What about this?' Rosie said, once we'd sat down. She was flicking through a tattered copy of *The Wizard of Oz*. 'One of us could be the Tin Man and the other could be the Scarecrow.'

'Hmm,' I said dubiously. 'Can't you just imagine what Macaroni would say?' I mimicked Macaroni's simpering voice. 'Ooh, Alex! What a great idea. You look so much like a scarecrow already, you hardly have to do a thing!'

'Then I'll be the Scarecrow and you can be the Tin Man,' said Rosie.

'I think I've already proved how bad a tin costume would be, Rosie,' I said glumly.

'Oh, yes . . . See what you mean,' Rosie agreed.

After lunch, everyone was talking about their chosen costume idea for the Winter Parade – which didn't make Rosie and me feel any better. Miss Westrop said we could spend the whole afternoon on our designs once our maths projects were finished.

Lots of people had made a start on their costumes over the weekend, and there were bags and boxes of stuff everywhere. Mary Connor was making a grass skirt out of yellow wool, and flowered headdress out of circles of scrunched-up tissue paper. And Michael Pond and Mark Bourne were making capes and masks for their Batman and Robin costumes.

I buried my head in my maths questions and pretended to be finding them very hard work. Rosie had finished hers and was leafing through another stack of storybooks that Miss Westrop had borrowed from Class 5, looking miserable.

Just then, Miss Westrop held up some patterns and large pieces of fabric. 'Some kind parents have donated these,' she said. 'So if you need a basic shape for your costume – a robe or a top and trousers – come and see me.'

Rosie went up to get a pattern from Miss Westrop. 'Just in case,' she whispered to me.

'Oh, you've got an idea, then?' said Macaroni as Rosie passed her on the way back to her desk.

'I might have,' Rosie replied crisply.

'Ah, that's a "no", then.' Macaroni smirked. The fan club tittered, gathered around her as usual. Then she turned to me. 'So, Alex, what's your latest bright idea?'

I looked pointedly at my maths book. 'I'm *trying* to get my project done, Pearl,' I replied.

'Ooohh! I've never seen you so interested in maths before, Alex.' Macaroni giggled. The fan club fell about. 'Never mind, I'm sure you'll come up with an idea in the end. Perhaps I'll have something left over from mine that you can have . . .'

She reached into a big cloth bag and pulled out a design board. It had little squares of cloth pinned down one side, and some beautiful drawings of a long white gown. Not Macaroni's own work, that was for sure. 'I'm going to be an Ice Princess,' she announced proudly.

'Wow! Ooh!' breathed the fan club.

A little crowd formed. 'What's that, Pearl? Show us, go on . . .' As if she needed any encouragement to show off.

Miss Westrop came over to see what the fuss was all about. 'Pearl, who did this for you?' she asked, taking the board. You could see she was torn between wanting to disapprove and wanting to see more of the drawings.

'Well, as my mother used to be a model . . .' Macaroni began.

The whole class groaned.

Macaroni took no notice. 'Amber still has contacts in the fashion world, of course, and one of her friends – Giovanni Petrochio, you may have heard of him? He's a famous Italian designer – is helping me to design my costume. Giovanni has some amazing ideas . . .'

'So I see,' breathed Miss Westrop. 'Pearl, I'm not sure it's quite in the spirit of the thing to have a professional designer working for you . . .'

'Oh, but I'll be doing a lot of the work myself,' said Macaroni hurriedly. 'And you did say we could get help outside school, didn't you?'

'Well, yes,' said Miss Westrop.

'Can I help it if my help happens to be Giovanni Petrochio?' Macaroni twisted her perfect mouth into a triumphant smile. 'Amber said you'd be pleased. She said you might want to use Giovanni's work to show everyone how a *professional* designer works.'

'There is that to it,' said Miss Westrop thoughtfully. A little gleam came into her eye – the teacher gleam. The mustn't-miss-an-opportunity gleam. 'Yes, what a good idea,' she said finally. 'Gather round, Class Six. Perhaps Pearl can explain the process so far.'

Pearl laid the board on the art table and pulled some more drawings out of her bag.

Miss Westrop spread them out for us all to see. 'This is very educational,' she said. 'You're lucky, Class Six. Not many people get the chance to see how a top designer works. It's exciting, isn't it?'

We all murmured politely. The fan club twittered in agreement.

'Amber will do my make-up, of course,' Macaroni continued. 'She has so much experience. And my hair will be done by Irina

Brazilia,' she finished triumphantly.

We all looked blank.

Pearl sighed. 'Irina Brazilia is one of the top hairdressers at the television studios in town. She does loads of the celebrities and special guests on daytime chat shows. She was once even booked to be the assistant hairdresser to Madonna's reserve hair stylist.'

'Wow! She met Madonna,' exclaimed one of the fan club.

'Almost. Unfortunately, Irina went down with a tummy bug on the day of filming. It may have been a plot by a jealous junior assistant. But there was never any proof.'

Rosie and I rolled our eyes at each other.

'It all sounds very glamorous,' said Miss Westrop.

Macaroni nodded smugly. Then she looked at Rosie and me and suddenly said, 'But I'm sure Alex and Rosie must have some really amazing costume ideas too . . .' She smiled a sugary, deadly smile. 'I can't wait to see them . . .'

'Well, girls, that sounds very intriguing.' Miss Westrop smiled encouragingly. Then she must have noticed our hunted-rabbit expressions because she said, 'Right, let's hear how everyone *else* is getting on with their costumes!'

Everyone else started to talk at once.

'It sounds like some very good ideas are on the boil here,' Miss Westrop finished, after what seemed like ages later. 'And we still have plenty of time,' she added, looking straight at me and Rosie. 'So no rush or panic, all right?'

No rush, no panic.

And no ideas for my glittering career as a fashion designer!

Chapter Four

Before long, there were only a few days left until the judging of the Class 6 costumes – and neither Rosie nor I had even decided what to be yet. So now it *was* time to panic! After my first spurt of inspiration had gone down so badly, my genius had limped off and not come back. And to make it worse, our mums were even beginning to talk about 'helping us' with ideas.

Rosie's mum, Charmaine, was sitting in the kitchen with my mum. They were drinking coffee and hogging the biscuit tin. Evan the Terrible had been driving us all mad, wearing the elf hat he'd made at school –

shaking his head around so that the bell on the end of it would ring. In the end, Mum had bribed him to be quiet with a new video she'd bought on special offer and had hidden for just such an emergency.

Rosie and I had finished our measly ration of two biccies each, so we decided a change of scene might help. We went up to my bedroom and sat gloomily on my bedroom floor.

'If we don't come up with something soon,' I said, 'we'll just have to think of an excuse for not being in the parade. A tummy bug on the day?'

Rosie shook her head. 'No good. That won't get us out of the rehearsal. And we can't both be sick on rehearsal day and then again on the actual parade day.'

'We can if we stay near Macaroni Barconi,' I muttered. 'Listening to her rant on about her Ice Princess costume is enough to make *anyone* sick. Come on, we've looked at all my books, but Evan's got loads of picture books in his room. Let's go and get them.' Luckily, Evan was still glued to the *Peter Pan* video.

Some of the books had lovely pictures in them. In *Tales of Ancient Egypt* Rosie found a picture of a girl carrying a water urn on her shoulder. 'That looks really elegant,' she said, pointing to the girl's long white robe.

'Simple, but effective,' I agreed. 'Let's give it a go!' I threw my duvet on the floor, grabbed the sheet from my mattress and handed it to her.

I could just imagine me throwing amazing outfits together like this for the rich and famous . . .

'Oh no, Alex, what am I going to do? The photo shoot is in an hour and I have nothing to wear! My luggage got lost and I can't be photographed in Hiya! *magazine wearing this old tracksuit!' cries Honey Lalonde, the A-list movie star I'm a stylist for.*

'Not to worry, Honey. I can just throw something together from what we've got around here . . . Let's see, I'll turn this velvet curtain into a halter-neck dress and we can use the tassels as earrings!' I reply calmly to my distressed celebrity client.

'Oh, Alex, you're the best! What would I do without you? By the way, can I wear this outfit to the Oscars? No one else will have one like it!' says a delighted Honey.

'Of course you can! That's what I'm here for –

to provide some truly original style . . .'

'What do you think, Alex?' Rosie asked, grinning at me. She folded and twisted the sheet round her body like the gown in the book.

'You look brilliant!' I said, snapping out of my daydream. 'Ooh, wait. I've got another idea.'

I hurried her down to the dining room and took Mum's big white vase from its shelf on the dresser. 'Here, put this on your shoulder and practise walking,' I said. 'You need to get the movement right.'

Rosie took the vase and perched it on her shoulder.

'Head up, eyes straight ahead,' I instructed.

'But I won't be able to see where I'm putting my feet,' said Rosie.

I scanned the room quickly. 'No probs – there's nothing in your way,' I replied. 'Off you go. Just walk in a straight line. Make it as smooth and flowing as you can.'

'Right,' said Rosie. 'Smooth and flowing.' She put her head up, straightened her back, steadied the urn on her shoulder and moved across the room. Her first three steps were perfect . . .

If I hadn't been concentrating so hard I

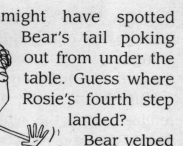

might have spotted Bear's tail poking out from under the table. Guess where Rosie's fourth step landed?

Bear yelped and scrambled upright. Rosie yelped and lost her balance. Mum's precious, expensive vase sailed through the air. When I saw it, *I* yelped and heaved myself, goalie-style, across the room to catch it. But Bear ran into my path and I fell right over him. We both yelped again – while the vase carried on arcing through the air to hit the door and smash, sending a shower of white china splinters everywhere.

A second later, the door was flung open. Mum stood there, with Charmaine close behind her.

Charmaine peered over Mum's shoulder and groaned. 'What have you girls done now?'

'What on earth . . .?' Bits of vase crunched under Mum's foot as she stepped into the room.

'Sorry, Mum – it was an accident!' I said quickly. 'It was part of the costume – Rosie was going to be an Ancient Egyptian. Look!' I thrust the book towards her.

Mum didn't look, because she suddenly realized what the white splinters were. 'My vase! Who said you could use my vase?'

'No one,' I had to admit. 'Sorry, I should have asked, but I thought you wouldn't mind. It's just like the urn . . .' I moved the book nearer to her face.

She pushed it away. 'Alexandra, I'm going to dock your pocket money until that vase is paid for. Now go and get a dustpan and brush and clear this mess up.' Then she marched out of the room. 'And don't think I haven't seen that chewed-up slipper, Bear. Bad dog!' she called over her shoulder.

Bear slunk back under the table guiltily.

'I'll speak to you later, Rosanna,' Charmaine said grimly, and then swept after Mum.

'Sorry, Alex,' said Rosie. 'I'm the one who dropped the vase. I'll help you pay it off.'

'It wasn't your fault, it was Bear's,' I said,

and looked disapprovingly under the table. Bear's soulful brown eyes stared out at me. 'If you had any pocket money, I'd be docking it,' I said sternly.

Bear whined, then wriggled out from under the table on his tummy and dropped a wet, slobbery chewed slipper at my feet as a peace offering. It was one of the slippers that Granny had bought Dad for Christmas. Dad had never liked them anyway.

'Oh, come here,' I said, and gave Bear a hug. His tail thumped happily on the floor.

'I think we'd better start again,' Rosie said as we swept up the mess. 'Let's forget the Ancient Egypt idea. Better not to remind your mum what happened.'

When we'd finished cleaning up, we trudged out to the kitchen. Evan sat there with a biscuit in one hand and a mug of milk in the other. 'Mummy says you made a mess,' he said happily. He nodded his head to make his elfin bell ring.

Rosie and I ignored him.

'Ooh, glum faces,' said Dad, wandering into the kitchen with his usual empty mug. 'Anything to do with that almighty crash I heard?' He started to fill the kettle.

'Don't ask,' I groaned.

Dad shrugged, then padded over to the biscuit tin. His face fell as he looked inside. He held up the remaining half a biscuit.

'We could go to Mrs Runce's,' I said helpfully. 'She'll still be open.'

'Good idea,' said Dad, and he handed me some money. 'Let me know when you've come back and made a pot of tea to go with them, would you?' He wandered out again, clutching the scraggy biscuit piece.

I rolled my eyes, wondering what kind of costume a tea-making slave would wear.

Mrs Runce beamed at us from behind her counter. 'Oh dear. You both look like you've lost a pound and found a penny. What's the matter?' she asked.

Gloomily, Rosie and I explained our situation. Mrs Runce knows the Barconi family, so she understood exactly how bad it was when I finished with, 'And the worst thing is, Macaroni . . . Pearl, I mean, is having this amazing costume specially made by an Italian designer.'

Mrs Runce handed over a couple of chocolates from the huge tin she kept under the counter, then popped one into her own mouth.

We all chewed in silence.

'I know!' she said suddenly. 'I should have thought of it straight away. Satin Smooth Delights.'

Rosie and I looked at her with puzzled frowns.

'Some time ago,' Mrs Runce explained, 'there was a big advertising campaign by Satin Smooth Chocolates. They gave shops that stocked Satin Smooth Delights special window displays. I'm one of their valued customers, as it happens,' she added, popping another chocolate in her mouth. 'So they came and did a wonderful display for me. They draped all sorts of beautiful fabrics across the window, with jewelled ribbons and everything.' She sighed. 'It was lovely. You should have seen it – too young to remember, I suppose.'

'Yes, I'm afraid so,' said Rosie politely.

'The thing is,' Mrs Runce sucked her teeth thoughtfully, 'somewhere upstairs I've still got all that fabric. It was so pretty I couldn't bear to throw it out. Did I tell you, by the way, that I'm going to be in the Winter Parade myself?'

'No, who with?' I asked.

'I'm going to be on the Derrington Dieters float,' Mrs Runce grinned. 'I've been a member of the Derrington Dieters for more than twenty years now.'

It was difficult to picture Mrs Runce on any kind of diet. I tried to imagine a diet that allowed you to eat chocolate whenever you wanted to.

'Of course,' said Mrs Runce, 'I've never lost more than about three pounds. People like me, we have big bones.' Thoughtfully, she swallowed the remains of the chocolate in her mouth and unwrapped another one. 'I'm the "Before", by the way.'

Rosie and I must have looked confused.

'For the parade,' Mrs Runce explained. 'Before and After. Me on one side and a stick insect on the other, showing how you should look *after* you've joined the Derrington Dieters.'

She slid off her stool and squeezed herself out from behind the counter, then slipped the *Closed* sign on the door and locked it. 'Come with me,' she said. 'It's just about closing time anyway. Let's go and find you those lovely fabrics.'

We followed her up the stairs and into her spare bedroom where there were two wardrobes and several wicker chests.

'This one, I think,' she said. 'Ah, yes.' She swung open one of the chests and lifted out its contents. 'I think you might find something here. Dive in.'

The fabrics that spilled out of the chest were lovely.

Rosie pulled out some pale-pink silky fabric

edged with gold. 'What about this?' she breathed.

'That was for a summer display for strawberry creams,' explained Mrs Runce.

Rosie twisted the pink and gold silk round herself. 'I feel like Cinderella going to the ball in this.' She laughed as she did a twirl. 'In fact, I think that's who I'll be. Problem solved! For me, anyway.' She did another twirl and smiled happily.

'Rosie, it looks great,' I began carefully, 'but I don't think you'll get very far in the competition as Cinderella. I don't think it will be imaginative enough.'

Rosie shrugged. 'I don't care. I've always wanted to dress up as Cinderella and now's my chance.'

'You'll make a beautiful Cinderella, dear,' said Mrs Runce. Then she turned to me. 'What about you, Alex?'

One of the fabrics shimmered and caught my eye. I pulled it out from among the others – it was a length of white silky material, with tiny glass beads and silver sequins sewn into it to catch the light.

'Oh yes,' said Mrs Runce. 'That's from the Christmas display for coconut ice. It looked like a glistening snow scene in the shop window . . .' She draped the fabric over my shoulders and stood back to look. 'Ooh, lovely . . .'

Mrs Runce's comment got me thinking, in a world-famous-designer kind of way. 'Hey!' I shouted. 'Who could be better to lead a Winter Parade than the Snow Queen?'

Rosie and Mrs Runce beamed at me in agreement.

'That's you two sorted, then,' Mrs Runce said happily.

Things were looking better and better. Rosie and I rushed home, full of hope and chocolate. Macaroni Barconi might not get her own way this time after all. Not if we could help it anyway.

'You two look happier,' said Dad when we got back. 'What biscuits did you get?'

Whoops.

Chapter Five

'*Ladies and gentlemen, may I present our new Princess of Fashion, Miss Alexandra Bond . . .*'

I smile. 'Call me Alex.'

'*Alex . . .*' *the presenter beams back. 'You're considered the most stylish young woman in the world. You've been elected the first Fashion Princess of the whole fashion and cosmetics industry. How does that feel?'*

I toss back my hair and smile my famous glittering smile. 'I'm just me, and I'm grateful that people find something in me that they like. For too many years, when I was young –' The camera moves in on me, looking sad and wistful – 'I worried all the time about my looks. Freckles, mousy-coloured hair and glasses were frowned upon then. I had all three. There seemed no future for me in the world of fashion.' I smile ruefully and spread my arms. 'And yet, here I am! If glasses are now trendy and young girls are proud of their freckles and mousy, flyaway hair because of me, then I'm happy too.'

'Alex, I'd like to shake your hand.' The presenter smiles.

He reaches over, grabs hold of my hair and pulls, hard . . .

'Ow! Evan, what are you doing?'

Another rude awakening. One of these days I'll finish a dream and find out how famous I really am.

Apparently not today.

Evan had a handful of my hair and was tugging on it. 'Wake up! Snow!' He jumped off my bed and pulled back the curtains. The light was dazzling and I could just see the tops of snowy trees.

I dashed to the window. 'Enough for the sledge!' I shouted.

I grabbed the first lot of clothes I could get my hands on – no time to worry about whether things were clean, or matched – shouted out to Mum and Dad that we were off to the park, then hurried downstairs.

As I pulled on my boots, I noticed that Evan had his cowboy suit on and was pulling his boots on to his bare feet. 'Evan! You won't be warm enough in that!' I said. 'And where are your socks?'

'I'm a cowboy,' he said. 'Cowboys don't get cold.'

'Cowboys don't get taken on the sledge either,' I said, and dragged him back upstairs to find some proper clothes.

Bear followed us, wagging his huge tail. He knew something was happening, but didn't know what.

'It's snow, Bear!' I said. We all charged back down the stairs. I opened the back door and, when Bear saw the snow himself, he went mad and started barking like crazy. Bear loves snow as much as we do. Dad says it's because he's a Newfoundland, and comes from a place where it snows a lot!

I headed through the snow to the garden shed where we keep the sledge and pulled it out. Then I took the dog harness off its hook. 'Here we go, Bear,' I said.

Bear stopped running about and jumping and stood perfectly still while I put the harness on him. Dad has trained Bear to pull the sledge, and he loves it.

When we were ready, Evan scrambled on to the sledge and I opened the gate. Bear stood patiently, like Dad had trained him, while I hopped on behind Evan. 'Walk on, Bear!' I called, and off we went.

Rosie was waiting for us, already dressed for sledging. 'I knew you'd be over with Bear and the sledge as soon as you saw the snow!' she said excitedly. 'Hey, do you want to see my costume first? Mum helped me get started on it last night.'

'No, we want to get to the park!' wailed Evan.

But I went in to see Rosie's costume anyway, and left Evan hopping up and down impatiently at the bottom of the stairs.

'Wow!' I said. Rosie's mum had used one of Rosie's dresses as a pattern to cut out a new dress from the pink fabric, except the Cinderella dress was long – to Rosie's ankles. It was still full of pins holding the pieces together, waiting to be sewn, but it shimmered pink and gold and looked lovely.

'Mum is going to weave lots of plaits into my hair, with ribbons to match – and I'm going to carry this.' She held up one glass slipper. 'I found it in the toy chest,' she explained. 'I could only find one, but that's OK.' She grinned. 'It'll be as if I've just left the other one at the ball for Prince Charming to find.'

'Brilliant!' I agreed. 'You'll look amazing!'

Rosie laughed. 'Hope so. But what about you?'

'I'm going to work on mine tonight,' I said. 'Mum's going to help me later, but you can't waste a good morning's sledging, can you?'

'We've got to go, right now!' Evan yelled up the stairs. 'The snow is melting already!'

'Well, come on, then!' I yelled back. 'We've waited for you long enough, Evan Bond!' Rosie and I giggled at his confused face. 'Let's go sledging!' I said, and pulled him outside.

Bear, who is not allowed in Rosie's house because whenever he wags his tail he knocks over her little sisters, was waiting patiently outside, still harnessed to the sledge. He jumped up joyfully and gave a big woof when he saw us.

Bear pulled Evan on the sledge, and me and

Rosie jogged along beside them throwing snowballs at any of our friends we happened to pass. (And a few were 'accidentally' lobbed at people we didn't even know, which is always good fun.)

Mr and Mrs Ranjay, our neighbours, were already in the park with their dog, Baron. He's only a little terrier and Bear could eat him in two mouthfuls, but fortunately they like each other. Baron came bounding over, barking at the sight of the sledge and running in circles, inviting Bear to play. But Bear stayed calm, just as Dad has taught him to when he's harnessed to the sledge.

'Hello, kids. Bear *is* enjoying himself, isn't he?' smiled Mrs Ranjay as she clipped a lead on to Baron's collar. 'He's very impressive with your sledge.'

'He loves it,' I said.

'Don't look now,' breathed Rosie. 'Amber Alert!'

I looked, of course. Bearing down on us, in a fur coat and stiletto boots that were about the worst thing to wear in snow you could imagine, was Amber Barconi. She was carrying a tiny white poodle that was shivering, even though it was dressed in a

tartan coat and strange little dog
bootees.

'Good morning!' called Mrs
Ranjay. 'How's your dog
enjoying the snow?'

'Not at all, I'm afraid,' sighed
Amber, with a sad smile. 'Poor
little Precious is terrified,
aren't you, darling? She's
never seen snow before, and
I thought it would be fun.'
Amber shivered and pulled her
coat closer to her with her spare
hand.

Mr Ranjay bent down and
patted Bear's big head. 'You love it, though,
don't you, Bear?'

Bear wagged his hefty tail and gave his loud,
deep bark. Precious jumped and whined.

'There, there, Precious,' soothed Amber.
'That big, ugly old dog isn't going to hurt you.
Mummy will protect you.'

Rosie and I looked at each other. Amber
Barconi won't even let *Pearl* call her Mummy.
So how come the *dog* is allowed to?

Amber looked disapprovingly at Bear. 'He *is*
under control, isn't he, Alison?'

'Yes, of course he is,' I said indignantly. 'And it's *Alex*.' Then an idea struck me. I looked at Precious, pretending to be concerned. 'Except . . .'

Amber clutched Precious to her. 'Except what?'

'Well,' I went on, 'cute little Priceless does look a bit like a toy . . .'

'An annoying squeaky toy . . .' Rosie whispered.

'Her name is *Precious*,' corrected Amber.

'The thing is,' I said, 'Bear has a toy just like Priceless, and he might fancy giving her a bit of a chew . . .'

Amber squealed and backed away, but Mr and Mrs Ranjay laughed.

'She's only joking, Mrs Barconi,' said Mr Ranjay. 'You can see how well-trained Bear is. In fact –' Mr Ranjay smiled at me – 'Mrs Ranjay and I were thinking that maybe we should ask Alex's parents if Bear could take part in the Winter Parade. The committee's already decided that the leader of the parade will be carried along on a sledge. I've been asked to design special wheels and springs that will make it easy to pull if there's no snow on the day. What a sight, if there were a proper working Newfoundland pulling it! What do you think, Mrs Barconi?'

Amber didn't look too happy about the idea. But I was! I thought it was a fantastic idea.

'But, Mr Ranjay, we decided at the last committee meeting that we would have two children in polar-bear costumes to pull the sledge,' said Amber.

'That was before we saw Bear,' said Mrs Ranjay firmly. 'We will have to ask the rest of the committee, of course, what they think. But I'm sure they'll agree – if Alex thinks Bear would be up to it?'

'Up to it? He would absolutely love it!' I grinned.

'But Pearl is very nervous of big dogs,' Amber protested.

'Well, Pearl won't have to go near him, will she?' I said.

'She will if she wins,' said Amber, her eyes glinting.

'I think we can cross that bridge if we come to it,' said Mrs Ranjay. 'After all, we can't be sure who will win, can we?'

Amber gave a hard little laugh. 'No, of course we can't. Well, I will, of course, bow to the will of the committee. I only want what's best for the school.' She gave Bear – and me – one last angry glare and marched off, wobbling on her heels in the uneven snow and clutching a whimpering Precious under her arm.

Mum was very excited when I told her. 'Right at the front of the parade,' she cooed. 'Clever old Bear! We'd better get you down to the Pooch Parlour so that you'll look your best.'

Bear slunk away before Mum could carry out this terrible threat.

In the afternoon, Mum and I got out the fabric Mrs Runce had given me and we cut out a simple robe shape then tacked it together. I only pricked my finger three times, which was very good, for me.

Mum found three whole rolls of silver snowflake ribbon left over from Christmas –

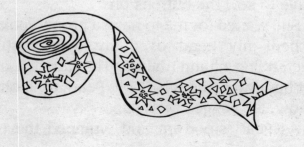

enough to sew round the neck and hem, for some extra sparkle, and put them in a bag. I couldn't wait to get to school for our next design lesson. One in the eye for Macaroni.

The next day at school, Miss Westrop said everyone could work on their costumes as soon as their history worksheets were finished. Rosie and I raced through in record time.

Macaroni was right there at my elbow as I unpacked my robe. 'Hmm, what's that, Alex?' she asked. 'A pair of old curtains?'

I ignored her.

She pulled her own design bag across the table and took out a gorgeous, shimmering piece of silver cloth, along with two buttons that looked like enormous diamonds. 'My Ice Princess cloak,' she explained loudly, although nobody had asked her. 'Almost finished. I just have to sew the buttons on.'

She waited for me to have a proper look, but I bent my head over my own costume, pretending I hadn't heard. The fan club didn't let her down, though. 'Ooh, Pearl, try it on and show us,' begged Melissa.

As Pearl stood up and wrapped the cloak

round herself, I looked out of the corner of my eye, still pretending not to be interested. It was lovely. She would be hard to beat.

'Pearl, did you make that cloak yourself?' asked Miss Westrop suspiciously.

'I had a little bit of help,' Pearl replied airily. 'But look –' she held out the buttons and a threaded needle – 'I'm doing a lot of it by myself as well.'

'Just remember that it's not the most professional, or the most expensive costume that will win,' said Miss Westrop. 'The judges will be looking for effort as well.'

'Yes, Miss Westrop,' said Macaroni meekly.

But as Miss Westrop turned away, she looked over at the fan club and smirked.

By the end of the lesson we all knew exactly how much work Macaroni must  have put into the costume herself. Almost zero! It took her ages to sew on the two buttons.

'Know a lot about sewing, Pearl?' Rosie asked.

'Enough,' said Pearl. 'Why?' she added suspiciously.

'Try doing up those buttons,' said Rosie.

Macaroni fiddled with the buttons and wailed, 'Oh no!' She'd sewn them on the wrong side.

Rosie held up her small scissors. 'Want to borrow these, Pearl?' she asked innocently.

Macaroni flounced off to sympathetic cooing from the fan club.

Unlike Pearl, I worked hard all afternoon on my costume, and that evening Mum helped me finish it off.

Dad got tea ready and did the washing up. 'Team effort,' he said.

By bedtime, my costume was just about ready.

'Try it on, then,' said Mum, smiling proudly as she helped me get into it. 'But be careful – this fabric is quite delicate.'

'Oh yes!' said Dad when I walked into the living room. 'Well done, Alex.'

I rushed over to see for myself in the hall mirror. The gown shimmered and rustled as I moved. Admittedly, scruffy purple trainers and a shimmery white gown didn't quite go together. My freckles were still there, my glasses had slid halfway down my nose and there was a smear of something mysterious on my cheek. But somehow I looked taller – almost elegant! And once my hair was in one of Rosie's special French plaits . . . I could already see me, about to lead the parade.

'Do you like it?' asked Mum.

'Like it? I love it!' I said happily, giving her a hug.

'Now listen, Alex,' Mum warned me again as she helped me out of the costume. 'No charging about in it tomorrow – and no wild games, OK?'

'As if I would!' I said indignantly.

'Yes, as if . . .' repeated Dad, winking at Mum.

'I don't know what you mean,' I said hotly. I took the costume and headed for the stairs before he could elaborate.

I did intend to go straight to sleep, honestly I did. But what possible harm could there be in one last twirl? Downstairs the telly was on. Mum and Dad were watching a detective film. Drinks and snacks were laid out on the table; they wouldn't move from the sofa until the end. Quickly – but very carefully – I slipped the costume back on and grabbed my sparkly hairbrush. With a bit of imagination, it made a reasonable wand. Yes, there she was, looking back at me from the mirror – the Snow Queen . . .

'You, a mere Ice Princess, dare to try and make people believe you are more powerful, more beautiful than me!' the Snow Queen accuses frostily.

'Forgive me, Your Majesty!' wails the Ice Princess. She sinks to her knees.

'I don't know how I could have been so stupid . . .'

'Why should I show mercy to you? Tell me why you think you deserve it,' the Snow Queen demands.

The Ice Princess bows her head. 'I deserve nothing,' she says sadly. 'I have been spiteful and proud. But now, I bow to your power, oh, Queen!'

'Quite right!' the Snow Queen agrees. 'You must show the proper respect, or it will be the worse for you. Now, how shall you be punished for your insulting remarks and haughty ways?'

'Oh, have mercy. Oh, Your Majesty, I beg you!' the Ice Princess pleads.

The Snow Queen considers, waving her wand thoughtfully. 'Very well, I shall be merciful this time, Ice Princess. But do not try the patience of the Snow Queen again.'

The wand moves in an arc over the Ice Princess's head. There is a flash of white light, but nothing seems to have happened. She staggers to her feet. The Queen has not turned her to stone.

'Thank you, Your Majesty,' she says timidly, and she bows several times in gratitude as she fades into the distance.

Only when she looks into a mirror and sees the two huge boils on her nose does she understand that she has not left the Snow Queen's presence unpunished.

Her terrible wailing fills the air; a deep dark echo rumbles through the underground palace, like a huge barking dog . . .

'Woof!'

'Bear? Bear, get off!' I yelled. He had nudged open the door when I was mid-spell. Seeing me waving something stick-like, he'd thought it was a game. And as I hadn't thrown the hairbrush for him to retrieve, he decided it must be tug of war.

Bear launched himself at the hairbrush. His front paws reached my shoulders and I toppled over. Bear tried to grab the brush's handle – but got a mouthful of dress instead. There was an awful ripping sound. I looked down in horror to see the skirt was all torn and some of the stitches at the waist had come undone. Bear reached again for the brush.

'Bear! No! Get OFF!' With all my might, I heaved him off the dress. A part of the skirt came away and somehow got wrapped round Bear's head. Confused, he charged about the room, the white fabric flying behind him like a strange doggy wedding veil.

Finally, I managed to grab his collar and make him stop. 'Bear, lie down!' I commanded.

Bear lay down, but looked up at me with a very disapproving expression, as if to say, 'I'm not playing this game again. It isn't much fun.'

I looked down at my ruined gown, all covered in doggy saliva and hairs. The Snow Queen had gone. In her place was a ripped, rumpled and drool-covered girl – more Ragged Street Urchin than Snow Queen. This wasn't good.

Chapter Six

I couldn't believe it. What was I going to do *now*?

Bear shoved his snout into my face and started licking me.

I pushed him away and he slunk over to the doorway and slumped across it. At least no one would be able to get in easily.

Slowly, I took my costume off and, thinking hard, put it on its hanger.

I weighed up my choices. The most obvious one was to go downstairs and tell Mum and Dad. I would interrupt their film – probably just before the ending so they'd be cross before they even heard what happened.

Who was I kidding? That was not an option. I was already paying for the broken vase with my pocket money. They would ground me until I was old and wrinkled.

I got out my mobile phone and texted Rosie.

Help! Costume ruined!

Rosie is a light sleeper and keeps her phone switched on by the bed, so I knew the bleeper would wake her up. Almost straight away I got a message back.

I'll help u fix it 2moro. Don't worry.

Don't worry? That was a bit like telling someone to duck when a rhinoceros is charging at them. But there wasn't anything else I could do now.

I laid the costume on the bed and folded it with the bodice on the top, so that you couldn't see much of the skirt. I did it as carefully as I could, otherwise Mum might decide to pull it out and do it 'properly'. Then I laid it on top of my chest of drawers, climbed into bed without even brushing my teeth, and closed my eyes.

'And next we have the lovely Alex Bond in one of her own divine creations. Even in those huge, purple platform shoes she's walking smoothly, gracefully down the catwalk. All the other top designers wanted her to model for them too, but

she just doesn't have time now she's the most popular young designer in the world.

'She's seen here in a simple white silk dress accompanied by . . . what kind of creature is that? It looks like a huge black-and-white dog – but it's jumping up at her . . . Oh no, she's beginning to lose her balance on those shoes . . . Oh, Alex! Down she goes!'

Thump! I fell out of bed and hit the bedroom floor.

It was morning, and Evan was singing at the top of his voice – practising his class's 'Elf Anthem' for the Winter Parade. He was already wearing his annoying hat. I could hear it ringing, even from my room.

He reached the end of the song and started again. I imagined him in his room, doing all the actions:

'We are elves, the mischief makers,
'We are secret baby wakers,
'We will make things disappear,
'Didn't I just put it here?'

The singing became a bellow as Evan got to the chorus:

'Elves are merry, elves are clever,
'Elves will be around forev-er!'

I sighed, steeling myself for the next verse. But just then, Mum came into the room.

'Time to get up, Alex,' she said. 'Oh, you're already up. Where's your costume?' she asked.

I scrambled to my feet and nervously pointed to the top of my chest of drawers. I know, I should have confessed there and then – honesty is always the best policy – but somehow, I always seem to forget that when I'm in a scrape . . . 'I folded it ready to take to school myself, because I knew you'd be really busy this morning,' I lied.

'Thanks, Alex,' Mum said, sounding pleased. 'I'll just find a bag for us to put it in.'

'Don't worry, I'll do that too, Mum,' I said hastily.

'Mum!' Evan's voice interrupted us. 'Come and see this spider. You've got to let me keep this one, Mum. It's huge!'

'Not again!' Mum sighed, and she went off to deal with Evan.

I sighed too – with relief. I listened at the doorway.

'Evan, house spiders are not pets. It's not staying.'

'But, Mummy,' wailed Evan. 'Look at him. He's sad and lonely. He wants a home. I can catch flies for him.'

'No, Evan. That spider is going out into the garden.' Mum went down the stairs with the spider trapped in a glass and Evan following closely behind.

It was a close shave, but I was in the clear. Mum would now be too busy dealing with the spider and consoling Evan over the loss of his new best friend. With a bit of luck, she wouldn't think about the costume again.

Rosie was waiting for me in front of her house, carrying her costume in a small suitcase. 'Let's have a look at yours, then,' she said. 'So what exactly did you do to it?'

I took the costume out of its bag and laid it over my arm. It still looked lovely, glittering in the morning sunlight. Maybe Rosie could help me find something at school to decorate over the ripped bits so that nobody would know.

I held the costume up against me and stepped back so that Rosie could take in the full effect – then skidded on a bit of ice hiding in the grey slush.

'Watch out!' called Rosie. 'Oh no!'

My poor costume, already torn and dribbled on by Bear, slid to the ground. I tried to grab it, but I lost my balance and fell on top, grinding it even further into the slush.

Rosie helped me up. We both stood absolutely still and silent, looking down at the costume. Not only was it torn, it was now also soaked and filthy.

'Never mind,' Rosie consoled me. 'Maybe we can . . . er . . .'

I stared at her hopefully. Rosie always tries to look on the bright side. You can count on her to come up with something comforting.

'We can . . . er . . . put it on the cloakroom radiator when we get to school and dry it out. It'll be fine . . . I expect . . .' she finished lamely.

Chapter Seven

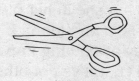

The playground was full of people carrying their costumes. Mr Manick, the school caretaker, was in full bossy broom-wielding flow. 'Move along there! I can't clear up unless you get out of the way. This is supposed to be a Litter Watch Zone, you know!'

'Oh, good morning, Mr . . . er . . .' called a familiar voice. Everyone turned round to stare at Amber Barconi, who was striding across the playground towards Mr Manick with a posh-looking dress carrier over her arm. Pearl was trailing along behind her, followed by the fan club who looked completely starstruck. Rosie and I rolled our eyes at each other.

'I thought I should offer my fashion expertise at today's costume competition,' Amber told Mr Manick importantly. 'I'm just on my way to see Miss Ross – is she in her office?'

'Yes, she is,' Mr Manick replied, still sweeping away at nothing in particular. 'But I can't stay and chat. I've got other things to do as well as judging the costume competition, you know!'

Amber's mouth fell open. '*You're* on the panel of judges, Mr . . . er . . .?'

'Manick!' Mr Manick snapped.

'Yes, I can see . . .' said Amber, looking a bit flustered.

Mr Manick smoothed his hair proudly. 'Miss Ross invited me 'erself.'

'That's right,' said Miss Ross, who had quietly joined the group. 'When Mr Ranjay found out last night that he'd be unable to attend the judging this afternoon, Mr Manick very kindly agreed to take his place.'

Looking very pleased with himself, Mr Manick nodded and brushed some imaginary dust off his overalls, then carried on with his Litter Watch.

Miss Ross turned to Amber. 'How nice to see you again so soon, Mrs Barconi. What can I do for you?'

Amber smiled graciously. 'I think it's more a question of what *I* can do for *you*, Miss Ross,' she said. 'As you know, I have considerable experience in these matters, and I have judged competitions like today's on several occasions . . .' she went on.

'Ah, I see. But isn't Pearl going to enter today's competition?' Miss Ross asked her.

Mother and daughter exchanged knowing smiles. 'Of course,' said Amber.

'Then, as I'm sure you'll understand, we couldn't possibly have you on the judging panel,' said Miss Ross smoothly. And before Amber could reply, she went on: 'But since you're here . . . Mrs Swaisland is in charge of decorating the school hall and I'm sure she would welcome advice from someone with your expertise. Could I impose . . .? Thank you so much. I think you'll find her in the staffroom.'

Amber's smile didn't look so fabulous through clenched teeth, but nobody argues with Miss Ross. 'Of course,' she said, and followed Miss Ross over to the hall.

Rosie looked at Pearl's scowling face. 'Result,' she said.

Rosie and I hovered about in the cloakroom until everyone had hung their coats up and gone into the classroom. Then we draped my poor bedraggled costume over the radiator.

After the register, Miss Westrop explained what was going to happen at the costume competition. 'Girls, you will go to the cloakroom to put on your costumes; boys, you will get changed here in the classroom. When the judging starts, you'll walk up the middle of the hall and on to the stage. The juniors will vote for the costume they think is the most imaginative. Their votes will be counted in with those of the judging panel, and the person with the most votes will be our winner and will lead the parade. So, let's get started.'

'I don't much fancy parading up and down the hall in front of everyone,' said Rosie as the girls lined up.

'You'll look great,' I said encouragingly. 'Which is more than I can say for me. Oh well, time to find out how bad it really is.'

'It'll be fine,' said Rosie kindly.

I knew, of course, that it would not be fine.

But I didn't realize quite how un-fine it would be until I saw myself in the loo mirrors.

As well as being filthy, the fabric had sort of shrivelled where it had got wet and the hole at the waist was even bigger now.

Rosie, who looked amazing in her lovely Cinderella costume, struggled to say something positive, but I could tell from the shocked look on her face that I was in trouble. 'It's a disaster, isn't it?' I said.

Rosie nodded, then hugged me.

'Help me get it off,' I said quickly. 'I'll just say I haven't got a costume . . .'

Too late.

'Ah, there you are, girls,' said Miss Westrop. 'Time to go into the hall. My word, Rosie, you look lovely. And Alex, you –' Her lips sort of froze for a second – 'you look very original . . . Forgive me, but I can't quite work out who you are supposed to be . . .'

'There was an accident,' I said quietly.

'I see,' said Miss Westrop. 'Alex, would you like to change back into your ordinary clothes and give the competition a miss?' she asked gently.

I was about to say yes and spare myself any further humiliation when, over Miss Westrop's shoulder, I saw Pearl's face. She was staring over at me, a delighted, malicious grin on her face. I was not going to give Macaroni the satisfaction of seeing me drop out!

'No, I'm entering,' I said defiantly.

'That's very honourable, Alex, but as who?' asked Miss Westrop.

'I'm going to be . . . I'm . . .' I looked at Rosie, who was almost in tears for me. I couldn't believe that, with Mrs Runce's beautiful fabric in tatters, my glittering career in fashion was ending before it had even begun. Suddenly, inspiration stuck. 'I'm going to be Cinderella,' I said.

'Ah. I see.' Miss Westrop still looked puzzled.

So did Rosie.

'Cinderella *before* the magic,' I explained. Then I pointed at Rosie. 'And Rosie is Cinderella *after* the magic. We're Before and After. Aren't we, Rosie?'

'Er, yes – yes, we are.' Rosie grinned. 'Just like Mrs Runce – and the "Before and After" Derrington Dieters' float,' she whispered to me.

Miss Westrop beamed. 'Very resourceful, Alex – well done! Right, let's get going.'

We all lined up. Rosie went behind me, so

that our new 'Before and After' theme worked. Macaroni and her fan club were giggling behind us.

'Just ignore them,' Rosie whispered to me.

But it was hard to, because Pearl did look amazing. Her Ice Princess gown had turned out to be awesome. It was made of stiff white silk that rustled when she moved. She had a high collar made of icicles, and there were more round her waist and the hem of the gown. They couldn't have been real ones, but they looked so lifelike that people kept reaching out to touch them. Her hair had been put up in a bun like a ballerina and sprayed with some sort of glittery stuff. She had very grown-up make-up on – and high heels too. I saw Miss Westrop frown at them.

The journey through the hall and up on to the stage felt like a very long one. I could see people staring and nudging each other as I passed. The worst thing was, I could hear them oohing and aahing at Macaroni behind me.

Up ahead, the judges were murmuring comments. Mr Manick had taken off his overalls and was dressed in an old-fashioned blue suit with two rows of buttons, a sparkling white shirt and a huge yellow tie. His hair was plastered on to his head with some very shiny grease.

'Who are you supposed to be?' he demanded of Cameron, the shyest boy in our class.

'I'm Prince Caspian,' said Cameron timidly. 'From the Narnia books,' he added.

'Never heard of him,' said Mr Manick scornfully.

'It's a very good costume, Cameron. Well done,' soothed Miss Ross.

The next two got through with just a disgusted look from Mr Manick, and a bit of muttering that I couldn't hear. Then it was Janny's turn.

'Who are you supposed to be, then?' Mr Manick asked, eyeing her up and down.

'Sleeping Beauty,' said Janny.

Mr Manick frowned, then put a big cross on his judging paper. 'How can you be Sleeping Beauty when you're awake?'

The rest of the judges fidgeted uncomfortably. Miss Ross shot Mr Manick a warning look.

Suddenly, he caught sight of me. 'Well, this one really takes the biscuit,' he said loudly.

'She's Cinderella,' said Rosie staunchly. 'Before the Fairy Godmother has done her magic. And I'm Cinderella after the magic.' Rosie is the best. She was so determined to stand up for me that she forgot to be shy.

'What a delightfully clever idea,' said Mrs Ranjay. She clapped, and a few other people joined in.

But Mr Manick wasn't impressed. 'I'm not sure even the Fairy Godmother is powerful enough to magic away *that* "Before" outfit.' He laughed.

'Mr Manick!' Miss Ross was stern now. 'That's enough,' she said firmly. 'Mr Manick, I must ask you to leave the panel. We shall manage without you.'

'You what?' said Mr Manick, looking shocked himself now.

'We have appreciated your help,' Miss Ross went on, 'but I have just realized your services are needed far more urgently elsewhere. Now would be a good time to make a start on polishing all the floors. We need them all *sparkling* for the Winter Fair, don't we?' She was using her don't-mess-with-me voice.

Mr Manick slunk off the stage and strode out of the hall, muttering to himself. 'Too sensitive by half . . . When I was a lad . . .'

After we'd all paraded up and down the hall we stood at the back with the rest of the school, fidgeting and chattering while the judges talked and swapped bits of paper and counted up. Finally, the announcement came.

'I am delighted to reveal that our Winter Parade will be led by Pearl Barconi, whose Ice Princess costume was judged the most . . . imaginative,' said Miss Ross, reading from a paper. You could tell she disapproved of Macaroni having done no work whatsoever! But the rest of the panel hadn't agreed, and neither had most of the kids in the hall.

Pearl didn't even bother to look surprised. She gave me and Rosie one of her most superior smiles and did a very princess-like curtsy. Everyone around us whooped and clapped. We had to smile and clap a bit too or we would have looked like bad losers. But if my smile looked anything like Rosie's, nobody would have been convinced.

I turned around, wanting to leave the hall and get out of my humiliating costume at the first possible moment, when the next bombshell dropped.

'And congratulations to Rosie Stevens and Alex Bond,' Miss Ross went on. 'They came joint second and third as our runners-up with their inspired idea of "Cinderella – Before and After".'

There was more applause. And a bit of laughter.

Rosie gasped and hugged me. 'Inspired idea!' she laughed. 'Did you hear that? Alex Bond, you are a champion, Olympic-standard, world-record-beating blagger!'

I suspected that, despite my top fashion redesign of the Snow Queen outfit into the 'Before' outfit, my mum still mourned all her hard work. After school the next day she invited Charmaine round to take a good, long, horrified look at my costume.

'Calling this . . . dirty rag . . . a "Before" Cinderella was very resourceful, Alex . . .' Charmaine concluded slowly.

'*My* costume's lovely,' said Evan, with a superior smile. '*I* haven't done *anything* silly, have I, Mummy? We all tried on our elf waistcoats at school today and Miss Ross says we look *just* like elves. *And* she likes our song. Shall I sing it for you?' He took a deep breath, opened his mouth and began. '*Elves are merry, elves are clever, elves will be around for–*'

'I fancy a chocolate biscuit to finish off my tea,' Dad interrupted hastily. 'Anyone else want one?'

And by the time Evan thought about being an elf again, I'd escaped.

Chapter Eight

O n Thursday, with just two days to go before the fair, Class 6 had a parade rehearsal in the playground. 'You will be leading the whole school, so it's important you know exactly what you're doing,' Miss Ross told us in assembly.

After lunch, we all trooped out to the playground with Miss Ross and Miss Westrop. Mr Manick was there too, as usual, waving his broom about and trying to be in charge. He told us where to stand, and then Miss Ross came along and moved us somewhere else.

Mum was there with Bear, who was very excited to find himself at school. He'd often tried to get through the gates but had never been allowed before, and he seemed determined to make the most of it. Class 5 were playing football in the school field next to the playground and he was straining to get nearer. Bear loved playing football – even more than pulling a sledge. But when he spotted Rosie and me, he forgot the game and strained towards us instead, wanting to say hello.

We went over and gave him a hug. The rest of the class crowded round to stroke him too. Bear loved it.

'Am I glad to see you.' Mum smiled. 'We needed a distraction from that football match.'

'Mr Manick, could you bring out the sledge, please?' called Miss Ross.

With great pride, Mr Manick opened the door of the sports-equipment store and slowly wheeled out the Winter Parade sledge.

'Wow! It's lovely!' I exclaimed.

'Look at all those flowers,' breathed Rosie.

The sledge was a bigger version of the one Bear was used to pulling, but this one had been decorated with white flowers and dark-green leaves, and covered in sparkling fake frost. It had a light, springy frame underneath with wheels on it. So even though the snow had almost gone, the sledge moved very smoothly along the ground.

Bear strained at his lead to investigate it for himself. Mum took him to have a good sniff around. I held my breath – usually when Bear stops to sniff things on a walk, he ends up widdling on them. But he seemed to know this would not win him any friends today, and the sledge stayed dry.

Miss Ross turned to talk to all of us. 'Now, Pearl will stand on the sledge, pulled by Bear. Alex and Rosie will walk directly behind, and then the rest of you fall in neatly in groups of three. After you will come the rest of the school, then the floats. Has everyone got that?'

Bear gave a loud bark, as if to say 'Yes'. Everyone laughed.

Miss Ross came over to us. 'We need to get Bear to set the pace: not too fast, but no sudden stops.'

'Let's give it a try,' Mum said, and buckled Bear into his harness. He wagged his tail in anticipation.

'Here you are, then.' Mum handed the lead to Pearl.

She took it reluctantly. 'I'd rather be pulled by the boys in polar-bear suits,' she said.

'Try to relax,' Mum advised. 'Bear will know if you're nervous and you'll make him jumpy too.'

'I'm not nervous,' said Macaroni, looking a bit pale. 'Why, what will he do? Will he stampede or something?'

'He's a dog, not a herd of cattle,' I said. I couldn't help being jealous that Macaroni, my sworn enemy, got to lead the Winter Parade with *my* dog. And she didn't even want him.

'Don't worry, everyone, I'm here!'

We all looked to see Amber Barconi half running across the playground towards us, carrying a cloak and Pearl's high-heeled shoes.

We had been told not to wear costumes, and Miss Westrop looked quite cross. 'Good afternoon, Mrs Barconi,' she said. 'You really shouldn't have –'

'Oh, I haven't brought the costume,' gushed Amber. 'Just a couple of rehearsal items to help Pearl get into the role. After all, the Ice

Princess will set the tone for the whole parade, won't she? It'll just take a second,' she said, handing the cloak and shoes to Macaroni.

'It's good of you to take such an interest, Mrs Barconi,' said Miss Ross coolly, 'but I wonder if I could ask you to leave us now? With the exception of Mrs Bond here, who has brought her dog, we didn't issue an invitation to parents to come to rehearsal . . .'

Miss Ross's disapproval penetrated even Amber's rhino-thick skin. 'Of course,' she said. I heard her giving Pearl some last-minute tips on embracing her inner Ice Princess before she hurried off like a naughty Class 1 child.

'Pearl, don't forget to hold on to the handrail,' said Miss Westrop as Pearl climbed on to the sledge. 'I know you'll only be going slowly, but hold on nonetheless, to stay safe.'

Macaroni nodded, but she wasn't really listening and was busy practising her royal wave.

Bear stood very still and steady as we all moved into final positions. But the football match had caught his attention again. Compared with standing around in the playground, it was obviously way more exciting. Suddenly, one of the Class 5 boys scored an unexpected goal. A huge cheer went up, and Bear took off like a rocket towards the football pitch, barking joyfully – on a mission to join in the fun.

The fan club stood, open-mouthed, as their Ice Princess jetted along the playground. 'Stop him, somebody!' they wailed, and 'Hang on, Pearl! Hang on!'

But with no hands, and wearing those high-heeled shoes, Macaroni didn't stand a chance. She slid to the floor of the sledge and just managed to grab a corner to stop herself from flying off.

I immediately started to run after them.

But by then, Bear had a pretty good head start.

Class 5 stared at Bear coming towards them, with me in hot pursuit, followed by

Mum and Rosie, Miss Ross and Miss Westrop – and the rest of Class 6. They whooped and cheered some more.

Bear, encouraged by the cheers, picked up speed. But just as he reached the football pitch, Mr Manick came in from the side, trying to head him off.

'Stop!' Mr Manick shouted, frantically waving his broom. 'Stop!'

Bear seemed to think that this was great fun – part of the chase. He swerved sharply to the right, making a sudden dash for a gap in the boundary hedge. Macaroni finally had to let go. She made a graceful arc in the air then landed in a muddy puddle right in the goal mouth, and slid into the back of the net.

'Goal!' shouted somebody. There was another loud cheer.

'Mum, you go to Macaroni, we'll get Bear!' I shouted, and Rosie and I charged off.

Bear was still running. But he misjudged the gap in the hedge and got stuck fast, his legs scrabbling wildly. I finally caught up with him and grabbed him by the collar. Rosie ran up to help me, and together we hauled him and the sledge out of the hedge.

'Bear, how could you?' I shouted. 'Naughty, naughty boy!'

Bear looked perplexed.

I caught hold of his lead. His tail was down and he looked very sorry for himself.

'Poor Bear,' said Rosie. 'He was just playing. He has no idea why we're shouting at him.'

'I know,' I said. 'But if Macaroni is hurt, it's not going to be much comfort that Bear didn't mean it. Come on, let's see how she is.'

We led a very sober Bear off towards the muddy goalmouth.

Pearl yelled when she saw Bear coming towards her, so we knew she was alive and that at least her voice was OK. Mum was leaning over her while Miss Ross hovered nervously nearby. We stopped where we were, so that Macaroni wouldn't scream again.

'I'm pretty sure nothing's broken,' Mum said a couple of minutes later. 'But we'd better get her to casualty, just to be on the safe side.'

Mum and Mr Manick made a chair with their hands and carried Pearl off to Miss Ross's car.

Miss Ross called everybody over. 'I'm going to take Pearl to the hospital to get her checked over. But as this is the only chance for a rehearsal we will have, I think everyone else should carry on. Miss Westrop, can you take over, please?' She strode off after Mum and Mr Manick.

'Alex,' said Miss Westrop, 'would you take Bear's lead and walk with him, please? We don't want to risk him running off again.'

Bear looked up at us and wagged his tail. He stood still and steady, the picture of innocence.

'He'll be fine,' I said, crossing my fingers. 'Come on, Bear.' I led him back to the playground.

'Rosie,' said Miss Westrop, 'we also need someone to ride on the sledge so that Bear gets used to pulling it and you came joint second in the competition, so up you go. Obviously we all hope that Pearl will be OK to ride in the sledge on Saturday – but if she isn't, you will be in her place.'

'Oh no!' gasped Rosie. 'I wouldn't want to be stared at. Let Alex do it, she loves that kind of thing.'

'We need Alex to keep Bear calm,' said Miss Westrop. 'You'll be fine, Rosie, stop worrying.' She was using her 'no nonsense' voice that showed she was losing patience. 'We have very little time left. Let's get on.'

The rest of the rehearsal went without a

hitch. With me leading him, Bear behaved beautifully. And Rosie got to lead the Winter Parade after all. Sort of.

Chapter Nine

Pearl wasn't in school the following morning. After Miss Westrop had taken the register she updated us. 'I have just spoken to Pearl's mother,' she beamed. 'You'll be relieved to hear that Pearl is all right, although she won't be in school today.'

The class cheered. It was hard to know whether this was relief that Macaroni was all right, or approval for the 'won't be in school' bit.

'Why not?' asked Rosie. 'Did she break something after all?'

'Goodness, no,' said Miss Westrop. 'She's bruised and shaken, and I'm afraid the fact that she wasn't holding on to the rail led to a minor whiplash injury when the sledge moved forward so suddenly.' Miss Westrop could not stop a tiny note of satisfaction creeping into her voice as she added, 'I did tell her to hold on.'

'Whiplash. You get that in your neck, don't you?' said Marlon. 'My dad had that when he crashed his car.'

'Yes,' said Miss Westrop. 'I gather Pearl will be wearing a neck brace for a few weeks. And unfortunately she twisted her ankle as well . . .'

'Not surprised, in those shoes,' I muttered.

Miss Westrop looked at me disapprovingly. 'Don't gloat, Alex.'

'What will happen about the Winter Parade?' I asked.

'Ah yes, the parade,' said Miss Westrop. 'Pearl will still be taking part – but not on the sledge.' She tried not to smile. 'Instead, Pearl is going to be on the hospital float, in their Accident Prevention display.' She silenced the gigglers with a stern look.

'So who will lead the parade, then, Miss?' one of the boys asked.

Miss Westrop turned to Rosie and me. 'Our joint-second winners,' she said. 'Rosie on the sledge, with Alex leading Bear.'

I looked at Rosie, who was sitting there, wide-eyed. 'Wow!' I said. 'That's great!' Then I remembered I'd be wearing my gruesome 'Before' Cinderella costume for everyone to see. Not so great.

The fan club were looking at me with daggers in their eyes. 'I bet she trained that dog to go mad,' muttered Natalie.

I went over to her and gave her my best evil stare. 'Maybe I did,' I murmured in her ear. 'And maybe I've trained him to do other stuff too. Why do you think we call him Bear?'

'Don't be stupid,' said Natalie. But she went satisfyingly pale, all the same.

Miss Westrop hadn't finished. 'Now, Amber Barconi has told a lot of magazines and newspapers that Pearl will be wearing a "Giovanni Petrochio original gown" to the parade,' she went on, with a disapproving little frown. 'A lot of them are sending photographers, and the committee has decided it would be a shame to lose such good publicity for the Winter Fair and for the school.' She smiled at Rosie. 'So, Rosie, as you are taking Pearl's place on the sledge, we'd like you to wear the Ice Princess costume.'

There was a small outbreak of enraged splutterings from the fan club. 'What? Well, honestly . . .' That sort of thing.

'Is that all right with you, Rosie?' Miss Westrop asked.

Rosie nodded and smiled back, looking anxious at the same time. I knew what it was: she was dying to wear the gorgeous Giovanni costume, but she hates being in the limelight.

I realized that I would look even more ridiculous now, with no 'After' Cinderella. But this was Rosie's big chance, and I didn't want to spoil it for her. I smiled as best I could but, inside, my stomach had sunk into my trainers. That awful costume of mine, on full display! Next to a 'Giovanni Petrochio original gown'.

But Rosie had already been thinking about that problem.

'Alex, why don't you wear my Cinderella costume for the parade?' she said as we swapped our sarnies at lunchtime. 'Mum says we can have a fancy-dress party for my birthday, so everyone can have a chance to wear their stuff again. I'll need it for that, but it's a shame not to use it for the parade, don't you think?'

'Rosie, you're a genius. Thanks!' I said, and gave her a hug.

After school, I picked up the costume from Rosie's house and dashed home.

'Hey, what's the rush?' asked Mum as I flew past her on the way to my room.

'Rosie's taking Macar– I mean, Pearl Barconi's place, costume and all. So I've got Rosie's Cinderella costume,' I said happily. 'I'm just going to try it on. It'll be great.'

'She's a good friend, your Rosie,' said Mum. 'I'm not sure I would lend you my costume, not with your track record.'

'Ha ha, Mum,' I said sarcastically. But not even Mum's comment could dampen my excitement at putting on Rosie's beautiful Cinderella dress.

As I step carefully on to the glittering sledge that is decorated to look like Cinderella's magical carriage, I can see camera flashes popping all around me as the photographers jostle for position to get the best picture of me for the papers and magazines. I am leading the Derrington Winter Parade, not just as Alex Bond, Class 6 student, but as Alexandra Bond, special celebrity guest! I am doing Derrington a favour – putting it on the map, so to speak – by appearing at the parade instead of jetting off to the runway shows in Paris. But I have a soft spot for the place where it all began, where my journey towards stardom started.

Yup, nothing could stop me feeling good . . .

Until I saw myself in Rosie's dress, that is.

I don't often think about how different we are, but the fact is I'm long and stringy, and Rosie is more rounded – and about twenty centimetres shorter . . .

So the dress that looked amazing on her looked stupid on me. It was too big in the middle and way too short. One shoulder kept slipping off, and my arms looked like sticks coming out of the armholes.

Disaster.

Cinderella? Hardly! Even the ugly stepsisters would have looked good next to me.

Chapter Ten

'A h . . .' said Mum, when she saw my disappointed face as I came downstairs. 'I did wonder whether it would fit, with you and Rosie being such different shapes.'

'It doesn't,' I said miserably.

Mum turned back to the carrots she was chopping. 'Never mind,' she said, throwing some slices into a pan.

'Never mind?' I spluttered. 'What am I going to do now?'

'You're going to do two things,' said Mum calmly. She finished the carrots and started on some broccoli. 'You're going to decide which of the two choices you now have will look the best.' She caught my expression.

'OK – the least worst.'

'What's the second thing?' I asked hopefully.

'You're going to learn that when I tell you not to mess with something, it's best to listen,' she said with a grin.

Grrrr. Mums.

'Alex, go and tear Evan away from that dratted *Peter Pan* video he's glued himself to again and make him wash his hands, please,' Mum went on. 'Dinner will be ready in a few minutes.'

It was Winter Fair chaos in our house after dinner. Mum was finishing off a banner for her float and filling little handout packs to give away. And Evan was practising the 'Elf Anthem' with all the actions. He insisted on wearing his elf hat too, complete with bell. So if the song didn't drive you completely mad after five minutes, the bell certainly did.

It seemed like I was the only one not entirely looking forward to the day. I had already decided that if I couldn't wear a paper bag over my head so nobody would recognize me, my life as one of the cool kids was completely over.

'Elves are merry, elves are clever,
'Elves will be around forev-er . . .'

OK, I had two choices. Gag him, or distract him. The first option was definitely the most attractive. The second would probably get me into less trouble, though watching Mum and Dad's expressions as he started up yet again, you couldn't be sure . . .

'Evan, my little elf brother,' I said, trying to sound all big-sisterly and friendly. 'Your "Elf Anthem" sounds so fantastic now, you don't want to overdo it. I've heard dreadful things can happen if you over-rehearse . . .'

Evan stopped singing immediately and his eyes went big and round. 'What like?' he demanded.

'Well . . . like forgetting every single word on the day . . .' I offered.

Evan clamped a hand over his mouth as if he wanted to hold all the words in. I felt a little bit guilty – but not much. It was great to be elf-free.

A couple of minutes later, the telly began to blare out. I recognized the opening bit of Evan's *Peter Pan* video. I decided to go and watch it myself – maybe it would take my mind off tomorrow's humiliation.

Evan was sitting on the sofa in his elf hat, eating a bag of crisps. Bear was sprawled at his feet, watching his every move in the hope that a crisp would end up on the floor.

I slumped down on the other end of the sofa and looked at the telly – then did a double take. On the screen, Peter was walking beside Nanna, the Newfoundland dog that helps look after the children in the story. On our sofa, a boy in a pointed green hat sat crunching crisps, being stared at by another Newfoundland . . .

My mind raced. Peter's costume could be quite simple. Green leggings, green T-shirt . . . I had some green woollen leggings somewhere and Mum had a green T-shirt. The only other thing I'd need was a hat like Evan's – but with a feather rather than a bell . . .

Inspiration had struck. Bear and I could lead the sledge as Peter Pan and Nanna!

I leaped off the sofa and gave Evan a big kiss. He gave a shocked 'Eurgghh!' and wiped his face – but I just laughed and charged off to find Mum.

'I love it!' she said, when I'd explained my idea. 'We could easily rustle up a maid's cap like Nanna's for Bear from one of my nurse's caps too. And that green T-shirt of mine with the pocket is pretty long, you know – when you've cut it to the right length you might even have enough material to make a matching hat.'

Mum dug out the T-shirt and she was right. I trimmed a few inches off the bottom and cut points into the new hem and the sleeves. When I pulled it in at the waist with a belt it looked just like Peter's tunic.

'What about shoes?' said Mum. 'Your school shoes and your purple trainers would just look –'

I thought for a second, and then beamed. More inspiration: 'My wellies are green!' I exclaimed, and Mum nodded with approval.

'Just the hat, then,' Mum said.

Carefully I cut round the pattern for Evan's hat, making it a bit bigger all round. And then I glued it together – no time for sewing.

'What you doing?' asked Evan, wandering in after the film had finished. He looked confused. 'Are you going to be an elf as well?'

'No, Evan, I'm going to be Peter Pan. Can't you tell?'

Evan thought hard. 'Well, sort of,' he said. 'But Peter Pan has a sword for fighting Captain Hook.' Then he went to the cupboard to get another packet of crisps while Mum was out of the kitchen.

I rolled my eyes and carried on with the final touches to my hat. Time to see the finished effect.

When I put it all together, it looked all right. Not brilliant, a bit rough and tatty, but three hundred times better than the 'Before' Cinderella wreck.

Just then, Evan came marching into my bedroom. 'Here, you need this,' he said importantly. He thrust his toy sword at me.

'Evan! You're a star!' I fitted it into the side of my belt. 'I owe you one!' I told him.

Evan backed away. 'No more kisses!'

Chapter Eleven

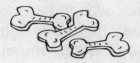

'Perfect parade weather,' said Dad at breakfast. 'Evan, you look a treat.'

Evan was wearing his elf costume. He kept lifting his feet to stare admiringly at his shiny black boots (painted wellies) and shaking his head to make the bell on his hat ring. Within ten minutes, that bell was driving us all equally as mad as the 'Elf Anthem'.

'Your costume's great too, Alex,' said Dad. 'Do you think you can make it up to the school without some disaster befalling you, or would you like us to carry you in a blanket, just in case?'

'Dad, you are *so-o-o* funny,' I said, grinning.

Bear looked great as well, with his coat all brushed and glossy and the little hat and apron Mum had made. Mum had tied them on with string.

We all walked to school together. Mum was in her nurse's uniform, ready for the hospital float. Bear padded along importantly in his outfit. I had my tunic pocket loaded with dog treats.

The sight that met our eyes when we reached school was amazing. People in all sorts of costumes milled about in between vans, floats and organizers wearing bright-yellow jackets. There were even a few policemen.

Evan was literally hopping with excitement, his bell ringing wildly.

We could hear people commenting as soon as we got near the crowd. 'Oh, look! Peter Pan and Nanna! Oh, see that? Aren't they cute?' I hoped the 'cute' was for Evan the Elf, but I was pleased that we were being noticed. A first step on the road to fame . . .

The fashion reporter quickly whips out her notebook and mobile phone. She calls the office of her magazine editor to tell her that she has the fashion scoop of the century. She has just spotted the Next Big Thing . . . and her name is Alex Bond. This girl, with her unique sense of style and winning personality, is going to be the hottest thing ever!

The insistent ringing of the bell on Evan's hat brought me back to reality with a ding-a-ling.

'Come on, Evan Elf, let's get you to your place,' said Mum. 'And then I'm off to find the hospital float, so I'll see you all later. Good luck, Alex.' Mum kissed me and then took Evan to find the other elves. Dad and I stood and watched all the noisy activity.

I scanned the crowd for Rosie, and finally saw her pushing her way through. I beamed. Macaroni's Ice Princess costume looked even better on her than it did on Macaroni.

'Wow! Look at you!' exclaimed Rosie. 'What a great idea. What happened to my Cinderella costume?' she added anxiously. 'Did you –'

'No, I didn't have any more accidents,' I grinned.

Rosie sighed with relief.

'The costume just didn't fit, so I had to dream up something else,' I explained.

'I know all about fitting problems,' said Rosie. She looked around to make sure nobody was watching, and lifted her cloak. Rosie was bigger than Pearl and it was clear that there had been no chance of zipping the dress up – across Rosie's back the whole thing was held together with hooks and rubber bands.

I laughed. 'Oh, Rosie!'

'Wait,' she said. 'There's more. What do you think Pearl would say about this?'

She lifted her robe just enough for us to see her feet. She was wearing her old red-and-white trainers. 'Those high-heeled things Pearl wore for the rehearsal were too small as well.' She grinned. 'It wasn't so easy to get round that one – I just couldn't squeeze my feet in them. I felt like one of Cinderella's ugly sisters, trying to get the glass slipper on!'

'Even so, Rosie, you look wonderful,' Dad said.

Rosie blushed and smiled shyly. 'Thanks, Mr Bond!'

'Yes, Macaroni will be sick as a pig when she sees you,' I added. 'You look so gorgeous, people will be gasping and needing first aid all along the street.'

Rosie laughed and shrugged her shoulders. 'I'm beginning to wish the parade was over and done with so I could just be in the crowd,' she added, sounding nervous.

'It's going to be great!' I said firmly, taking her by the arm. 'Let's go and find the rest of Class Six.'

Dad nodded. 'It's due to start very soon. Good luck, everybody.' He bent down to stroke Bear, whose tail was wagging very enthusiastically.

We moved off. It was then that I saw Macaroni on the hospital float. She was sitting in a wheelchair under the 'It can easily happen – take care!' banner, with her leg up and her neck brace on, looking very uncomfortable. She was wearing dark-green trousers and what looked like a specially made high-necked matching top that covered her neck brace. The choice of colour was unfortunate. Maybe if it hadn't been sludgy green, she wouldn't have looked *quite* so much like a giant bullfrog.

'Hi, Pearl,' I called cheerily. 'We're so sorry you missed out on being the Ice Princess. It must be awful.'

Macaroni looked Rosie over. 'You look all right, Rosie,' she said finally. 'Not as good as I would have, of course, but then Giovanni made it especially for me.' She sighed. 'I suppose I should be grateful that at least it wasn't given to the kind of person who would make anything look like a sack.' She gave me a meaningful look. 'Where did you get that Peter Pan costume, by the way? It looks awful,' she added.

'Actually, it's absolutely the latest look from Paris,' I said. 'I'm surprised at you, Macaroni. I'd have thought you would know . . .'

'And I suppose that dog of yours is Nanna, is it?' Macaroni scoffed. 'I thought Nanna was supposed to be a responsible, steady dog. Not like your . . . creature at all.'

'I can see you're suffering, Macaroni, so Bear and I will forgive you,' I said. 'To be honest, I would be grouchy in your shoes – sorry, sandals,' I corrected, looking at her swollen ankle swathed in bandages and topped with a granny-style open-toed shoe. 'I think you're really brave to join the parade at all. I'd be too embarrassed, looking like that.'

'Just go away!' wailed Macaroni.

Amber came over then and started fussing around her. 'Darling, just let me do your hair. You'll feel so much better if your hair –'

'Stop fussing, Amber,' Pearl snapped. 'Isn't it bad enough that I look such a frump?' She took the hairbrush and threw it on to the ground. 'Leave me alone!' Her scowl could have soured a glass of milk.

Looking annoyed, Amber lowered herself off the float – which, in a leopard-skin skirt as tight as hers, took some doing. She had matching shoes too.

'Ah, Alison, hello,' she said, seeing me.

'Alex,' I said. 'Short for Alexandra.'

'Yes,' she replied vaguely.

'Wow!' said a boy with a stick of candyfloss in his hand. 'Are those shoes really made from leopards, Miss?' he asked.

'No, of course not,' Amber snapped.

'They *look* like real fur,' said the smaller boy who was with him. He stepped forward to have a closer look.

Amber eyed his candyfloss, which looked decidedly crooked, and stepped back.

The bigger boy stuffed the remaining candyfloss in his mouth.

Amber breathed a sigh of relief.

And with no warning whatsoever, the smaller boy threw up all over Amber's feet.

Amber screamed, and Mum and the doctor jumped off the float in a flash.

'What's happened?' asked Mum.

Amber, too shocked to speak, pointed at her shoes.

'Oh no. Oh, you poor thing. Come on, let's get you sorted out,' Mum said.

Amber sighed and prepared to be helped out of her trauma by a sympathetic nurse. But then she realized that Mum was talking to the little boy who had thrown up, and was leading him away to the first-aid post.

The doctor climbed back on to the float, raising his eyebrows and muttering about hysterical females.

Rosie and I agreed that the Derrington Dieters was our favourite float. Mrs Runce looked brilliant. She wore a huge, full-skirted bright-blue dress and tight jacket to make her look as big as possible. She was on one side of the float, under the 'Before' banner. On the other side was a very thin woman, under 'After'.

Mrs Runce had rosy cheeks and a big beaming smile as she chomped her way

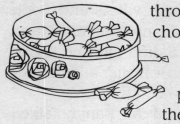

through the biggest tin of chocolates I have ever seen. Now and then she threw a handful to the people around her. But the thin woman huddled under the 'After' banner looked thoroughly cold and miserable.

'It's not exactly encouraging you to join, is it?' I said. 'You too can turn away from chocolate bliss to become thin and miserable like us.'

'Mmm, I see what you mean,' said Rosie, grinning.

'Five minutes! Positions, please!' came a voice from nowhere over the loudspeaker. The floats and people started to get into position and we hurried to the front of the parade.

Derrington School had turned out some brilliant costumes. The teachers were all characters from Winnie the Pooh. From time to time Tigger would call out, 'Keep the noise down, children,' or Pooh Bear would bellow, 'Keep in line there!' Only,

Tigger had Miss Westrop's voice, and Pooh Bear sounded like a slightly muffled Miss Ross.

'Pooh Bear's been on a diet!' giggled Rosie. It was true, Pooh looked a lot taller and thinner than usual.

The excitement mounted. Mr Ranjay talked to us all through a megaphone, telling people where to go.

As I buckled Bear into the sledge harness, I hoped I'd brought enough doggie treats to get through the day.

'We will go down Derrington Road and along Chaucer Avenue,' Mr Ranjay told us in his tinny megaphone voice, 'then through Perry Park, and back to school via Marlowe Road and Sheridan Road. Keep an eye on whoever's in front of you in order to help judge the speed. Right, everybody ready? Let's go!'

The parade started. There was a great cheer from the crowd as we slowly set off out of the school gates. I took a quick look behind me and saw a great stream of movement and colour.

All sorts of things were going on around us too – dancing girls from the theatre wiggled and smiled their way through the crowd wearing tiny yellow costumes and huge plumed headdresses. I wondered if they were cold, with no coats and not a lot of costume, or if they were so full of excitement they didn't notice.

'Let's see you fly, Peter Pan!' called someone from the crowd.

I smiled and waved. 'Maybe later!' I called back.

As we made our way through the streets, people pointed at Bear and me and clapped or even cheered! It was fantastic to be at the head of the parade, walking alongside Rosie on the Ice Princess sledge.

There were all types of music too: one of the  floats behind us carried a steel band, with players dressed in fantastic bright shirts. The Salvation Army brass band was marching in their dark uniforms. Another float carried a string quartet.

And then Class 1 began to sing the 'Elf Anthem'. The crowd was treated to the full, gruesome work – Evan's moment of glory had finally come. There were lots of 'aahs' from the crowd and one woman cried, 'Adorable, absolutely adorable!'

'She should have been staying at my house the last few days,' I called to Rosie.

'Oh, look! Peter Pan and Nanna! What a wonderful idea!' I heard someone else say, and I bowed – quite difficult to do, when you have to keep moving so the people behind don't bump into you.

'Halfway there . . .' I heard Rosie say and, when I looked at her, she grinned. 'It's not as bad as I thought,' she said.

Bear walked steadily and slowly, egged on with a steady supply of doggy treats. Whenever he felt a bit peckish he would take a sideways glance at my bulging pocket, then bark. He had me wrapped round his paw.

'Don't think this is going to happen every day, Bear,' I said as I fed him for what seemed like the hundredth time. 'This is a one-day offer only.'

Bear just wagged his tail.

When we reached Perry Park, some reporters and photographers came bounding over, their cameras flashing. 'Girls! This way . . . Girls! Over here.

Could you stand a bit closer together? Frank, make sure you get the dog in!' And so on. It was all very exciting!

Rosie and I stood side by side, with Bear in front of us, and let the photographers take a few pictures before we had to move on so the rest of the parade wouldn't pile into us. 'How does it feel to be wearing an original Giovanni Petrochio?' asked a reporter, thrusting a little tape recorder at us.

'Er . . . Great. Lovely,' mumbled Rosie.

'What about you, Miss?' someone said to me.

I looked down at my costume. Old T-shirt, too-small leggings, wellies – and a hat made of cardboard and leftover T-shirt . . . Naturally, I thought they were joking and I entered into the spirit of it. 'Giovanni's designs are always so fresh, so new,' I said, trying to sound as grown-up as possible. 'We're both really proud to wear anything by him, aren't we, Rosie?'

'Er, um, yes, of course we are,' said Rosie.

'But I feel especially lucky,' I said, trying to impress the reporters with my very grown-up witty humour, 'that I am wearing one of his *new* experimental designs.'

'What's this new style called?' asked a reporter.

'Shabby Peter,' I said. 'It's the very latest thing . . .'

Rosie was looking at me with her mouth open as the reporters murmured 'Ooh' and 'aah'. I winked at her as they wrote feverishly in their notebooks.

'Tell us about how you got your start, Alex,' asks the interviewer on Stars Today. *'Where did you get your big break?'*

'Well, I got my first break in my hometown of Derrington,' I reply. 'I was chosen to help lead the Winter Parade – with my dog and my best friend – and everyone just loved my inspired costume design. And I suppose that's where my love of design and costume started,' I say graciously. 'I've been designing and modelling my own creations ever since.'

'Wonderful!' says the interviewer, beaming.

By the time we got home, everyone was really tired. Bear headed straight for his rug, not even looking hopefully in his food bowl. Mind you, his stomach *was* full to bursting with doggy treats and hot dog.

Evan could barely keep his eyes open and had to be carried up to bed, but he was still singing. The words floated down the stairs as he drifted off to sleep.

'Elves are merry, elves are clever,
'Elves will be around forev-er!'

Elves may well be around forever, I reflected as I finished a fantastic day with my fingers in my ears, but the lives of little brothers who will not shut up are definitely shorter.

And for those who just have to know . . .

'Elf Anthem'
(an action song)

We are elves, the mischief makers,
(crouch down, look around furtively)

We are secret baby wakers,
(mime taking out a dummy and squawking)

We will make things disappear,
(spread arms as if mystified)

Solo: 'Didn't I just put it here?'
(look confused, scratch head)

Chorus: Elves are merry, elves are clever,
Elves will be around forever.

(Repeat chorus)

When it's Christmas we are good,
(put hands together in angel pose)

We help Santa chop the wood,
(mime chopping wood)

Then we help him make the toys,
(some mime using a hammer, some using a screwdriver)

For all the little girls and boys.
(let off party poppers and shout 'Hooray!')

(Repeat chorus)

But on the first of January,
(hold one finger up)

We're as naughty as can be.
(mischievous expressions, wave fingers in the air)

China breakers, baby wakers,
(mime throwing china on to the floor, or taking a baby's dummy)

We are elves, the mischief makers.
(crouch down, look around furtively)

(Repeat chorus)

An ordinary girl with EXTRAORDINARY plans!

Recipe for Disaster

Take:
- One ten-year-old girl with big plans
- One opportunity to appear on TV

Leave to marinate

An ordinary girl with EXTRAORDINARY plans!

Alexandra the Great

What's Cooking, Alex?

YVONNE COPPARD

Stir in:
- One oversized dog
- One gorgeous celebrity chef
- One arch-enemy

Bake at a high temperature

Serve with a big smile and hope for success!

Not Quite a Mermaid

Linda Chapman

You don't need a tail to make a splash!

Electra is different from other mermaids.
She has legs instead of a tail and is always getting
into scrapes in search of adventure!

Electra's class is having a competition to collect magic mermaid
fire from the seabed – the deeper you dive, the more you can find.
Will Electra and Splash be brave enough to dive to the very bottom?

puffin.co.uk

Lily Quench

Thirsty for a magical adventure?

Let Lily Quench it!

She's a feisty young dragon slayer and she's ready for action. Get ready for some scorching adventures in this exciting series.

lilyquench.com

What did readers think of Cathy's first book

'Cathy Cassidy is the new Jacqueline Wilson'
– Sarah, 13

'A hard-hitting, heart-warming, fun, exciting,
romantic, sad and gripping story.
I enjoyed this book so much that
I read it in three-and-a-half hours!'
– Katherine, 11

'I thought this was a fantastic story' – Sarah, 14

'*Dizzy* is a fabulous book.
Once I picked it up I couldn't put it down!'
– Jessica, 11

'I loved it' – Toni, 11

If you want to keep up to date with Cathy's latest news,
write to us at the address below:
Cathy Cassidy News, Puffin Marketing,
80 Strand, London WC2R 0RL